Charles Darwin

Alan Gibbons
Illustrated by Leo Brown

KINGFISHER
NEW YORK

KINGFISHER
LONDON & NEW YORK

Copyright © Kingfisher 2008
Text copyright © Alan Gibbons 2008
Illustration copyright © Leo Brown 2008
Published in the United States by Kingfisher,
175 Fifth Ave., New York, NY 10010
Kingfisher is an imprint of
Macmillan Children's Books, London.
All rights reserved.

Distributed in the U.S. by Macmillan,
175 Fifth Ave., New York, NY 10010

Library of Congress Cataloging-in-Publication Data has been applied for.

ISBN: 978-0-7534-6675-9

Kingfisher books are available for special promotions and premiums.
For details contact: Special Markets Department, Macmillan,
175 Fifth Ave., New York, NY 10010.

For more information, please visit www.kingfisherbooks.com

Printed in China
10 9 8 7 6 5 4 3 2 1
1TR/0511/LFG/SC/140M

Consultant: Professor James Secord, Cambridge University, U.K.,
Director of the Darwin Correspondence Project (www.darwinproject.ac.uk)

This is one of the surveying instruments that Darwin took on the Beagle voyage. The photographs in the diary chapter of this book show plants, creatures, and objects that Darwin saw during his travels.

Darwin preserved the animals that he caught in alcohol or chemicals in glass jars. These reptiles are part of his collection.

Contents

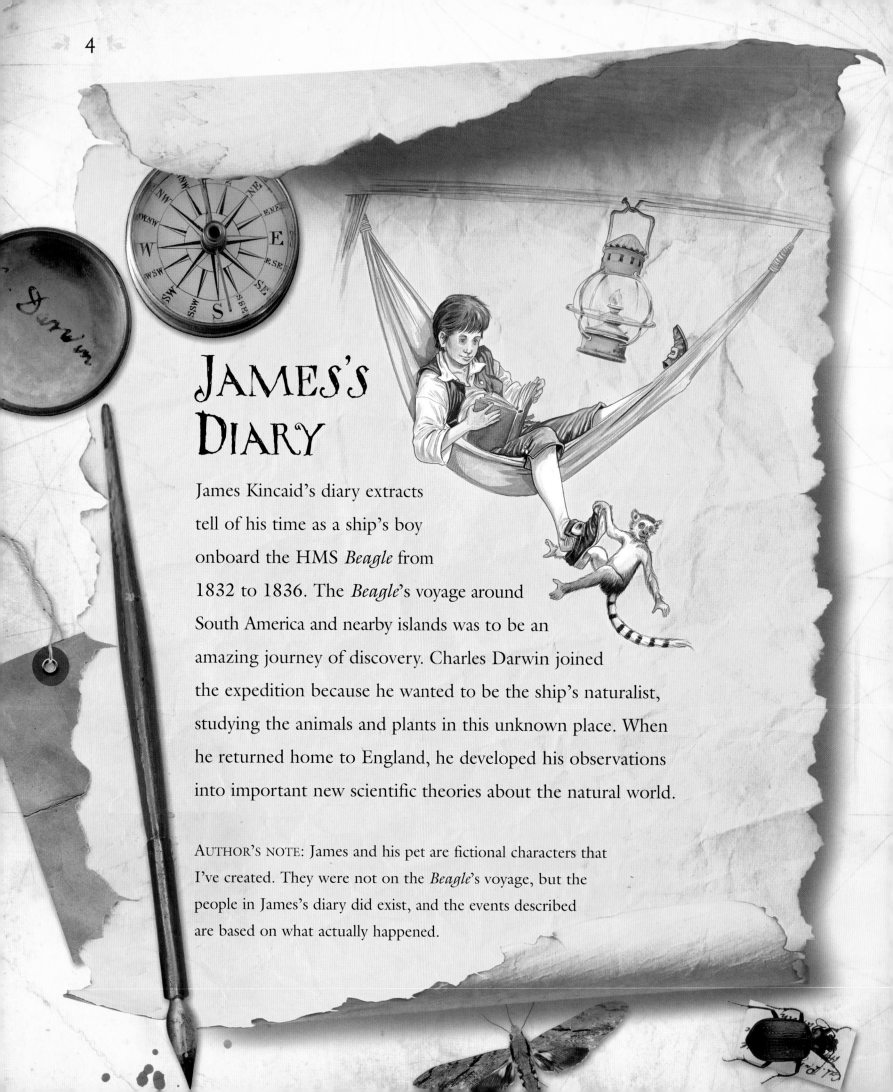

James's Diary

James Kincaid's diary extracts
tell of his time as a ship's boy
onboard the HMS *Beagle* from
1832 to 1836. The *Beagle*'s voyage around
South America and nearby islands was to be an
amazing journey of discovery. Charles Darwin joined
the expedition because he wanted to be the ship's naturalist,
studying the animals and plants in this unknown place. When
he returned home to England, he developed his observations
into important new scientific theories about the natural world.

AUTHOR'S NOTE: James and his pet are fictional characters that
I've created. They were not on the *Beagle*'s voyage, but the
people in James's diary did exist, and the events described
are based on what actually happened.

January, 1832

Today I received a gift. You may not think that's such a great surprise, but the man who gave it to me is a wealthy gentleman, and I am only a volunteer boy sailor and ten years old. My benefactor's name is Mr. Charles Darwin of Shrewsbury, England. Let me tell you how he came to present me with his gift—the journal in which I am writing this diary.

Our ship, the HMS *Beagle*, is several weeks out of Plymouth, England, on a journey to map and chart the coasts of South America and Tierra del Fuego, its southernmost point. The master of the vessel is Captain Robert Fitzroy. Mr. Darwin is traveling with us as his guest. This is the first time we have touched land since we set sail. The crew members are clearly glad to disembark and look around. Some are gathering fresh fruit to keep scurvy away.

MIDSHIPMAN KING

HMS *BEAGLE*

CHARLES DARWIN

CAPTAIN ROBERT FITZROY

JAMES KINCAID

Our present port of call is the island of St. Jago. It is located 450 miles from the coast of Africa. I have never seen a place like this. The land is very dry—we've been told that it hasn't rained for an entire year! Mr. Darwin looks most relieved to be walking on solid ground once again. By all accounts, he has had a terrible passage. Captain Fitzroy told his officers that the crossing of the Bay of Biscay was the worst he has experienced.

Mr. Darwin made notes about each bird that he saw on St. Jago.

Poor Mr. Darwin has spent most days rocking in his hammock, suffering dreadfully from seasickness. Midshipman King, who shares a cabin with him, says that he even clears off the cabin table sometimes so that he can lie flat. He has little experience of life at sea and has yet to find his sea legs.

But there is more to it than mere relief at setting foot on firm ground. Mr. Darwin seems thrilled by the lush green valleys, the coconut palms, and the orange trees that we see everywhere. How different this world is to the one we left at home.

I saw Mr. Darwin in the market this morning. He had just bought a banana and was sampling it. He didn't seem to know what to make of the taste at first. Finally, he decided that it was too sweet. Later in the day a flock of strange birds took flight, 50 or 60 of them in all. Mr. Darwin told me that they were guinea fowl. That was the first time he ever spoke to me. It wouldn't be the last during our stay on the island. Although I am no gentleman, he seems happy to involve me in his explorations.

Notebooks are essential for cataloging the discoveries during the journey.

We moved on to Quail Island. Mr. Darwin is collecting every creature that he can find. He says that walking around these tropical islands has been like giving a blind man eyes. He is starting to see the world in a different way. This afternoon he scoured the rock pools along the coast. He was incredibly excited by an octopus that he found. He watched with great wonder when it changed color as it tried to escape. He was soon scribbling down notes and sketches in a small book. He has amazing enthusiasm for nature's treasures.

To keep the octopus from rotting, Mr. Darwin preserved it in alcohol.

When he noticed me watching, he produced a second book from his pocket and offered it to me. He asked me if I knew how to read and write. When I told him very firmly that I did, he was pleased. He suggested that I keep my own diary of the voyage. Well, I protested strongly, saying that he shouldn't be giving his precious notebooks away to anyone and everyone, but he finally persuaded me to take it. Secretly, I am absolutely delighted to have it.

Back onboard the ship that night, he showed everybody how the octopus that he had captured could glow in the dark. He was like a child himself, thrilled by his find. He was most disappointed to hear that it wasn't a new discovery. Nonetheless, he is putting together his scientific discoveries, making notes, and cataloging his finds. For a man considering entering the Church when he returns to England, he seems set on a very different career. Surely he was born to be a man of science and exploration?

For the first time since I signed up for the voyage, I am beginning to feel at home. I have fallen in love with the ship. The *Beagle* is going to be my home for the next few years. She is 90 feet long with a capacity of 242 tons. She has three masts and a cannon. According to Captain Fitzroy, that makes her a ten-gun brig. Some of the men say that she is really little more than a wreck, a broken-down coastal carrier.

I don't care what they say. I love it when I am sent up to loosen the sails. It is so exhilarating to be high up above the deck with the wind in my face and the sea spray stinging my eyes! You can see far, far across the glittering ocean.

I expect the *Beagle* to introduce me to the most marvelous sights and adventures. Joining her crew wasn't such a difficult decision. I was orphaned some years ago and have been living with my uncle in Wapping, England, selling supplies to seafaring folk. My uncle and his wife have always considered me something of a burden, so I was glad to trade them for my new family, the crew of the *Beagle*.

In addition to the crew, there are others onboard. There is Mr. Darwin, of course. Captain Fitzroy chose him because he is a gentleman of good breeding and a suitable companion for the captain. Then there is an instrument maker, a missionary, and an artist. Because of these guests, the deck is covered in their boxes and instruments. The missionary, Mr. Richard Matthews, is charged with returning three natives, Fuegians from Tierra del Fuego, to their home at the tip of South America.

Captain Fitzroy brought the natives to England on a previous journey, and they have been living there for some time. They even had an audience with His Majesty the King and Queen Adelaide. I have seen the natives fleetingly from time to time, but I will write about them in greater detail when I know more about them.

As I lie here in my hammock, watching the oil lamp swinging back and forth, casting its yellow glow, I can hear the prow cutting through the waves, the snap of the wind in the sails, and the creak of the rigging. No doubt Mr. Darwin is suffering from seasickness again, but once he has recovered he will unearth more of nature's secrets. My hope is that he will let me accompany him.

It is our third day on the islands. Mr. Darwin has become fascinated by a horizontal white rock around 45 feet above the water. He believes that this layer is an old sand beach, raised up in the recent past by the force of a volcano. It cannot have been very long ago because the shells are just the same as the ones that we collected by the ocean today. In his mind's eye, Mr. Darwin seems able to see all the changes that the land has gone through. Later, he even showed me how the volcano had erupted, baking the seashells into the hard, white layer. How he can figure this out simply by looking at the hillside and examining the rocks and soil, I can't imagine, but with every day that passes he seems to become more sure of himself. He thinks that he can tell the story of the islands from these signs. Mr. Darwin is either very intelligent or very imaginative.

He was sitting on the beach eating tamarind fruit and crackers for lunch and gazing at the tidal pools at his feet, when he smiled suddenly. One of the men asked him what he was thinking. He said quietly that one day he was going to write a book about the natural history of the island.

February–July, 1832

Mr. Darwin collected a huge range of creatures in his nets, including many crabs.

The days continue to be warmer and the waves less choppy than when we crossed the Bay of Biscay. The sails ripple lazily in the gentle breeze. Mr. Darwin spends most of the day trawling the waters for plankton and jellyfish. He uses the most peculiar contraptions to catch his creatures and study them. I have rarely seen any man more excited about something as simple as fishing. When he is dipping for his samples, his eyes sparkle. He sometimes asks me how my diary is progressing. I tell him that I am keeping it up to date when I can, filling it with my thoughts and sketches. He seems pleased. Of course, I try not to take up too much

of his time. He is, after all, the captain's guest and a fine country gentleman. I have heard it said that he is related to Mr. Josiah Wedgwood, the famous potter. I have a feeling Captain Fitzroy would be most displeased if he thought that I was pestering Mr. Darwin. I must be respectful, or the captain will lose patience with me.

I have good reason to be wary of the captain. I remember my first experience of discipline at sea well. I was roused early in the voyage by the shrieks of sailors being flogged. The captain ordered that four men be lashed with the cat-o'-nine-tails. It cut their backs to shreds. It turned out

that they were being punished for drunkenness, insolence, and neglect of duty. Five others were clapped in shackles. The captain was sending out a message. He is prepared to handle the crew with a firm hand. Since that day I have been careful to do my duty well. I don't want to suffer a beating like those men. I still remember the look on Mr. Darwin's face as he watched the floggings. He was as disturbed as I was. It seems that we think alike about many things.

I have had a chance to observe the three Fuegians. All three of them are quite short in stature and copper-skinned. The oldest goes by the name of York Minster. Imagine being named after a church! His real name is El'leparu. He is a quiet, brooding type of man. He is very protective of the only female in the group, Fuegia Basket. Her real name is Yockushlu. She is very quiet in her ways but quick to learn languages. She has picked up English and some Spanish and Portuguese. The crew's favorite is Jemmy Button, also known as Orundellico. He is a gentle, fun-loving man who enjoys telling jokes. He is very proud of his English appearance, and he always dresses in smart London clothes. He wears his hair neatly cut and oiled.

It seems that the captain took them to England as a type of experiment. He wanted to see how they would adapt to English ways and how they would behave when they were returned to their own land. I have often heard Captain Fitzroy and Mr. Darwin discussing the Fuegians, debating how strong the influence of British society will prove to be. I can't help but wonder how they will be. How easy will it be for them to fit into their former world after so long away? What if they have gotten too used to our English ways? Still, our arrival in Tierra del Fuego is several months in the future. We will see what happens when we get there.

SHACKLES

JEMMY BUTTON

YORK MINSTER

FUEGIA BASKET

Very occasionally, the captain relaxes discipline a little. Today was an example. Mr. Darwin had to undergo quite an ordeal. It is called Crossing the Line. One of the crew painted himself green and pretended to be the sea god Neptune, the king of the deep. The youngest volunteers onboard, Musters and I, were done up in our own war paint. We pranced around while the other men egged us on. For just a few moments it didn't matter who were the officers and who were the men in their charge. The world had been turned upside down. We actually shaved some of the officers. We even poured buckets of salt water over the heads of Mr. Darwin and Captain Fitzroy, something that would have been unthinkable on any other day. It was great fun, but after an hour or so, of course, everything had gone back to normal, with the officers giving us orders and we obeying them without question.

The moment we arrived in Bahia, Brazil, Mr. Darwin was off on his travels. He sees the voyage of the *Beagle* less as a sea journey and more as a series of adventures on land connected by quick hops across the ocean. He came back, as he always does, with many specimens in his jars and boxes. There are beetles and spiders and the most brightly colored butterflies you've ever seen in your life. He seemed thrilled to be caught in a tropical rainstorm that soaked him through in seconds. He found the entire experience very exciting. He wants the lands that we explore to be as different from his native Shrewsbury as possible.

His high spirits didn't last long. He was soon horrified by the spectacle of slavery in the territories of Brazil. The slaves are flogged much more savagely than the sailors on the *Beagle* have ever been.

I already knew that Mr. Darwin was appalled by any type of cruelty. I've seen his face when the captain punishes members of the crew. It seems that the Darwin family are great opponents of the slave trade. Mr. Darwin believes that the poor wretches we saw shackled are men and women like the rest of us and have the same feelings as anyone else. Captain Fitzroy is of a different opinion. He believes that they are reasonably well treated and as happy as if they were free people. He can't see any difference between the slaves and the factory hands who work for Mr. Darwin's relative, Mr. Wedgwood, in his famous pottery factory.

This difference of opinion led to a furious argument one evening. We sailors could hear it up on deck. To our amazement, a whisper went around the ship the next morning that Captain Fitzroy had apologized for losing his temper. None of us had ever dreamed that a man as proud as the captain would apologize to anyone. It seems that the two gentlemen have agreed not to discuss slavery again so that they can avoid quarreling over the issue.

Mr. Darwin has seen a fish called a blenny. This is a drawing of it.

He is a very intelligent gentleman, although not so smart that he can't be caught out by the sailors' mischievous humor. On April Fool's Day one of them called out, "Darwin, did you ever see a Grampus?" Well, Mr. Darwin came rushing out on deck in great excitement, imagining that he was about to see some unknown species of animal, only to discover an empty sea. The crew had tremendous fun at his expense.

On the way from Bahia to Rio de Janeiro, we passed through a stretch of sea that was stained bright red. We all wondered about this strange sight until Mr. Darwin explained that the color came about because of millions of tiny creatures swimming around. No matter how hard I stared, I could see nothing but a crimson stain on the surface of the ocean.

When we docked in Rio de Janeiro, Captain Fitzroy ordered that the *Beagle* be caulked and painted in preparation for our onward journey. This would mean quite a long time onshore while repairs were carried out. During that time, Mr. Darwin rented a house nearby. From Rio, he has sent many boxes of specimens home to England. He certainly meant what he said about telling nature's story. It is a great task, but I think that Mr. Darwin will be up to it. He doesn't save everything for his collections, of course. One day he and Captain Fitzroy amused themselves by scrambling over the rocks on the seashore, killing sea birds for the pot. They killed many noddies and boobies. Mr. Darwin said that the birds were so stupid that they could have killed many more. I felt quite sorry for the poor creatures.

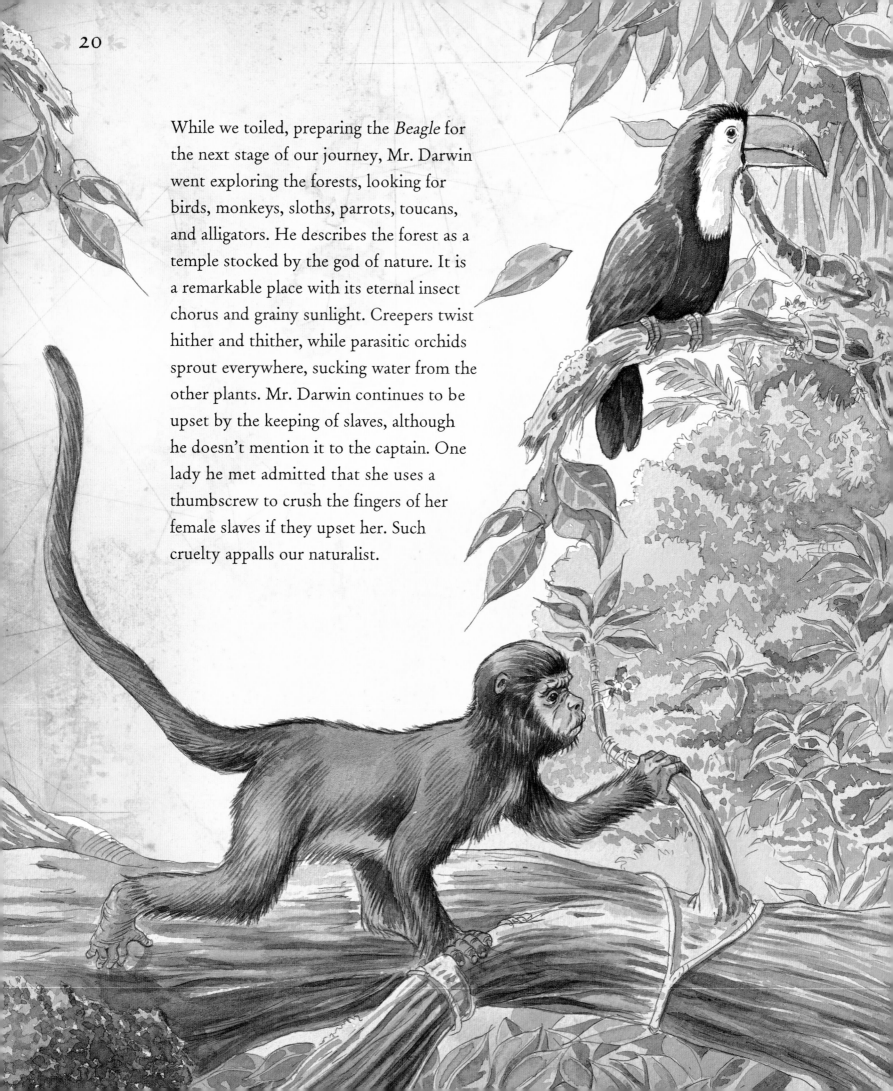

While we toiled, preparing the *Beagle* for the next stage of our journey, Mr. Darwin went exploring the forests, looking for birds, monkeys, sloths, parrots, toucans, and alligators. He describes the forest as a temple stocked by the god of nature. It is a remarkable place with its eternal insect chorus and grainy sunlight. Creepers twist hither and thither, while parasitic orchids sprout everywhere, sucking water from the other plants. Mr. Darwin continues to be upset by the keeping of slaves, although he doesn't mention it to the captain. One lady he met admitted that she uses a thumbscrew to crush the fingers of her female slaves if they upset her. Such cruelty appalls our naturalist.

July–August, 1832

The bola is two balls, one on each end of a rope. The balls are swung around and then thrown to wrap around a creature's legs and capture it.

We are at sea once again. Mr. Darwin's nets and trawl nets are everywhere, hanging over the side of the ship. He spends hours poring over his books, staring through his microscope, and making reams of notes, but something happened this afternoon that brought him up on deck in a hurry. We came across a school of porpoise. There were hundreds of them leaping over the waves, often jumping clear out of the water. There were times when you might think they could fly. They entertained us for several minutes, crisscrossing the sea in front of the bow. We were disappointed when they finally left us alone.

There was some excitement when we arrived in the harbor of Buenos Aires. A guard ship fired on us.

This was a sign of things to come. When we reached Bahía Blanca, we discovered that there was a lot of fighting between the Indians and an Argentine general, a ruthless man named de Rosas. It seems that his army is set on exterminating the Indians. It is said that they are even prepared to massacre women in cold blood!

War or no war, Mr. Darwin is continuing his studies of the land, the plants, and the animals of South America. He has been very fascinated by the local ostrich, the rhea. The horsemen, or gauchos, catch these flightless birds by flinging two balls held together by threads. Mr. Darwin had a try with the bola, as it is called. He swung it around his head just as he had seen the gauchos do. Unfortunately, he hadn't gotten the hang of the contraption and managed to catch his own horse in the process! The gauchos roared with laughter. They said that they had seen men catch all types of animals, but nobody had ever caught himself before. The incident was embarrassing, but it didn't put Mr. Darwin off hunting. The ship's crew have dined on fresh tuna, turtle, shark, and barracuda. We have also eaten deer, ostrich, and armadillo. Sometimes I think that Mr. Darwin prefers eating nature to telling its story!

August - November 1832

Mr. Darwin found many fossil bones. These are the foot bones of a Macrauchenia, which was a type of large llama that lived millions of years ago.

We have made a great discovery. Rounding a headland called Punta Alta yesterday, Captain Fitzroy and Mr. Darwin came across some broken bones and shells embedded in the gravel beds. The two men were soon digging furiously with their bare hands. The bones turned out to be fossils. The captain and his guest ordered several of us to return with them today to chip the fossil bones loose. Soon we uncovered the teeth and bones of several very strange animals, which Mr.

Darwin thinks were probably a type of rhinoceros from a bygone era. Looking at these fossils, it was obvious to everyone that these animals had to be extinct. We had seen nothing like them roaming the Argentine plains. The story of nature must be longer and more mysterious than I had imagined. Mr. Darwin seems to be puzzling over it. How can animals from past and present be so similar in some ways and so very different in others?

December 1832-January 1833

As we approached Tierra del Fuego, we witnessed some huge humpback whales churning the ocean. One whale leaped almost entirely clear of the waves. Later, an albatross wheeled above us. It was very graceful, content to ride the breeze, like some king of the skies.

As we approached the Fuegians' homeland, fires started to spring up. Soon we caught sight of the inhabitants running along the shore in great excitement. Their bodies were painted red and white, and they were hardly wearing a scrap of clothing. We looked first at the three Fuegians onboard, Jemmy Button, York Minster, and Fuegia Basket, then at these people following us. Mr. Darwin was fascinated that the three Fuegians could transform themselves into English citizens in such a short time. He is convinced that they will probably transform back again just as easily once they have been returned to the forest, an idea that upsets Captain Fitzroy. According to him, civilization is a very fragile thing indeed.

Jemmy has been reunited with his brother and mother, back in the land from which he came. That doesn't stop us from being very sad to leave the Fuegians in their homeland. They have been our companions ever since England. We will miss them greatly.

September 1833

I have just returned from an excursion inland. Captain Fitzroy allowed me to accompany Mr. Darwin on a long expedition across the pampas. It is wonderful to ride over the vast plains and sleep under the stars. We met General de Rosas and his gauchos along the way. The gauchos wear their hair long over the shoulders of their brightly colored clothes. When they walk around, their spurs jangle loudly. They never remove the daggers that poke out menacingly from their belts. They escorted us across one especially dangerous part of the pampas where we saw deer and ostrich. We roasted an ostrich one night and ate it around the campfire. We also discovered more fossil bones. Mr. Darwin said that they belonged to a Mastodon (an elephant-like creature), but sadly they were too soft and powdery to be removed from the earth. He spent several days wondering how some species died out while others seemed to thrive much longer.

Now that our time traveling across the immense, open plains is at an end, we are turning our minds once again to Tierra del Fuego. Captain Fitzroy intends to continue charting the coast while he makes his way back to the place where we left the Fuegians. He wishes to know how they have fared in the meantime, especially Jemmy Button, who was always the crew's favorite.

The gauchos' spurs are attached to their boot heels and are used to guide a horse when riding.

March 1834

On our return to Woollya Cove, where we last left the Fuegians, we saw three canoes approaching the *Beagle*. We did not recognize any of the occupants at first. Then one of them raised his hand to his head in a type of salute, and we realized that it was Jemmy Button. Captain Fitzroy and Mr. Darwin were dismayed to see that he had become very thin and was wearing native clothing— in other words, very little at all! Captain Fitzroy ordered that Jemmy be given some clothes so that he could eat at the captain's table like an English gentleman. Jemmy was soon using a knife and fork and acting like he had never been away.

Jemmy is now married. His wife came with him to meet us, accompanied by Jemmy's brother, known to everyone onboard the *Beagle* as Tommy Button. Before we left Woollya Cove for the last time, there was an exchange of gifts. The captain gave Jemmy a set of clothes, and Jemmy gave him some otter skins. For Mr. Darwin there were two spearheads. The entire crew lined up to shake Jemmy's hand as he said his farewells. As I watched his short figure vanish in the distance, I had a lump in my throat. We would all like to believe that one day some British seaman might crawl up on the shore after a shipwreck and find himself looking up into the smiling face of Jemmy Button.

TOMMY BUTTON   JEMMY BUTTON   JEMMY'S WIFE

July 1834 - June 1835

We have reached Chile. After our visit to Tierra del Fuego and the bleak Falkland Islands, the sight of the glittering Pacific Ocean, the bright sun, blue sky, and cloud-wreathed Andes lifts the spirits. As Mr. Darwin put it, nature is sparkling with life. The volcano of Aconcagua is huge, towering to a height of 23,000 feet. It is the highest peak in the Americas. It almost took my breath away. When you walk through the countryside, the flowers and shrubs give off wonderful perfumes. If you brush against a plant, your clothes will be scented with its aroma.

While we were surveying the nearby island of Chiloé, we witnessed a remarkable sight as three volcanoes erupted. At first all we could see was Mount Osorno spouting clouds of thick smoke. But there were more dramatic sights to come. The eruption lasted into the early hours of the following morning, and nobody onboard thought about going to bed that night.

If we thought that the havoc wrought by wild nature was at an end, we were wrong. A great earthquake has followed the eruption of the volcanoes. The earth started rocking and shuddering. The vibrations only lasted a matter of minutes, but the effects on the local towns and villages was devastating. When we visited the town of Concepción, most of the buildings were razed to the ground. Beautiful churches have crumbled away completely. The town was nothing but a mass of rubble and timbers. Enormous cracks and fissures mark the earth all around.

Mr. Darwin soon concluded that the earthquake had extended over an area of 400 miles and involved three volcanoes in total.

He set to work, spreading out his books and matching what he read there to his own information, gathered from what he had witnessed with his own eyes. He believes that the volcanoes in a single range are connected deep below the surface of Earth. Because they are linked, they will tend to erupt together or one after the other in sequence. He concludes that the ground is a crust resting on a sea of molten rock and that volcanoes are holes in the ground. When a volcano has been closed for some time by rock and dried lava, pressure builds up until there is a violent eruption.

I am becoming more and more interested in the story of the natural world. It seems ever-changing and often violent, and so much seems to be happening under the surface. Mr. Darwin describes it wonderfully and has a gift for gazing into nature's internal workings and explaining them. If he ever does write that book of his, I am sure it will be a great success.

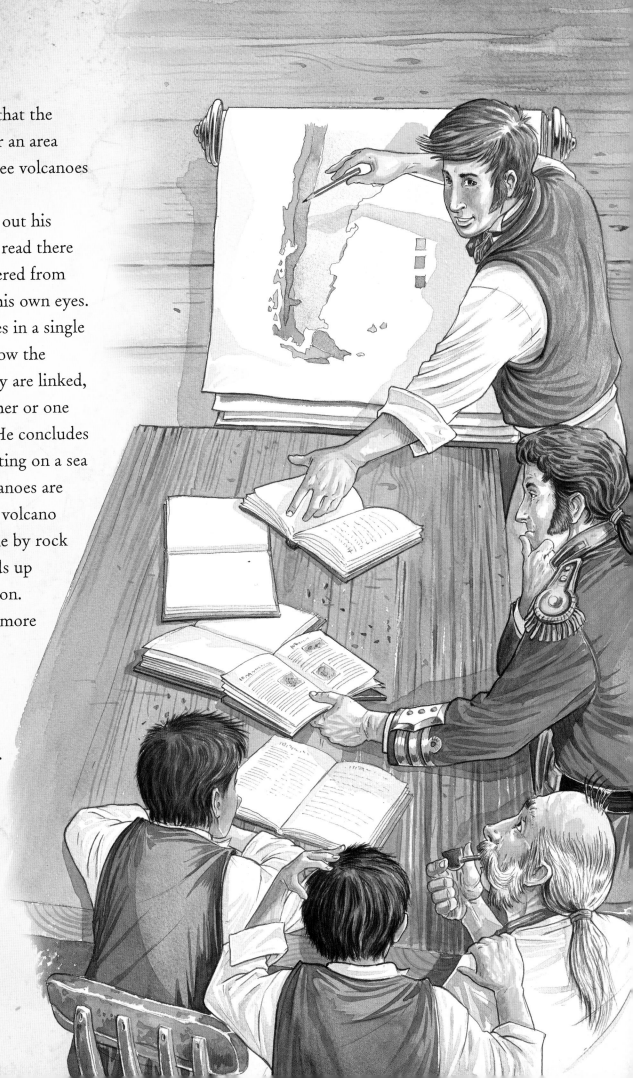

September 1835

We have left South America and are about to arrive in the Galápagos Islands. There are 15 of them altogether, 600 miles from the coast of Ecuador. They are all formed from volcanic rocks and straddle the equator. Mr. Darwin is delighted to be here. He says that the collection of islands is a perfect little world within itself. He is eagerly looking forward to exploring them more than anywhere else on our journey.

We landed in high surf today on the northeast coast of Chatham Island. We waded ashore through icy water, only for our clothes to be dried immediately by the morning heat once on land. To our surprise, everything here seems very dark. The beach is made of dark-colored lava. The land all around is jagged and buckled. The only vegetation is the stunted brushwood, scorched by the sun. Everywhere there are craters and steaming vents. It is like nothing I have ever seen before.

The barrenness of the land is deceptive. The sea around Chatham Island is swarming with fish, sharks, and turtles.

The crew have been enjoying themselves fishing. The birds are unaccustomed to human company here. They hop up very close, ignoring the pebbles that are being thrown at them. It is even possible to prod or catch them.

The birds have none of the wariness of the wild birds back in England.

One of the first land creatures we came across was the seagoing iguana. This creature swarms in its hundreds over the rocks. The iguana is very tame. It will put up with being prodded and poked. Mr. Darwin even picked up one of them, swung it around his head, and threw it into a rock pool. It just picked itself up again and waddled back to where it had been lying, settling itself back down as if nothing had happened. Mr. Darwin threw it back into the rock pool. When the creature returned a third time, he repeated the operation. Once more, the iguana plodded back to its place. Mr. Darwin concluded that, whereas European lizards have learned to fear people, these iguanas have failed to develop that hereditary instinct themselves. The iguana saw the side of the rock pool as a safe sanctuary so it kept returning to it, even though Mr. Darwin insisted on dumping it back in the pool. I am not sure that Captain Fitzroy would agree with Mr. Darwin's theory. He seems to distrust radical new ideas. But Mr. Darwin doesn't seem to have firmly made up his mind about his view of life on these islands, so I don't think that there will be any major arguments such as there were about slavery early in our voyage.

The smaller tortoises are around the size of a dinner plate, but others are the size of a table!

Some time later we came across the island's biggest inhabitants, the huge Galápagos tortoises. We had been trudging through the weedy vegetation when we came across a type of path between the cinders and the cacti. Turning down one of these paths, we finally met a pair of tortoises face to face. They must have weighed at least 200 pounds each. To hungry sailors that means 200 pounds of meat, of course. Many of these tortoises do end up in the pot, but not the pair we encountered on that particular day. We were more interested in them as living creatures. As we approached, one was eating a cactus. The other gave a grumpy hiss and walked away. I tried riding its back but, even though the tortoise didn't seem concerned at all or even aware that I was perched on its shell, I was unable to balance and kept slipping off and landing with a thump on my bottom. Midshipman King also had a turn at riding the tortoise, but he ended up sprawled in an embarrassed heap just like I did.

On Albermarle Island we came across a second species of iguana. In contrast to its cousin on Chatham Island, this is a land-based reptile. It is just as unaccustomed to people as the seagoing iguanas on Chatham Island. Mr. Darwin watched one of them burying itself in a burrow. When it was halfway underground, Mr. Darwin pulled its tail. The iguana emerged to see what was the matter. It clearly wanted to know what was impeding its progress and it stared hard at Mr. Darwin as if to say: What do you think you're doing? But it wasn't afraid. It hadn't yet learned to fear people.

James Island was the last island that we visited. Mr. Darwin was especially interested in the finches. Their habits were varied. Some of them survived on cacti, and some survived on insects and leaves. Some stayed on the ground, whereas others lived in the trees. Mr. Darwin had them all sketched. He would lay out the drawings and point out the way they all had beaks suited to their particular diet. Some had long, pointed beaks, whereas others had shorter, heavier ones. He sits watching the wildlife and smiling. As we sailed away from the islands, some of the officers told Mr. Darwin that they had seen different birds and tortoises on different islands. This has given him food for thought. He calls the Galápagos Islands the land that time forgot. I have a feeling it is a land he will remember all his life.

Mr. Darwin has preserved these reptiles in alcohol so that they won't rot on the long journey home.

November 1835

We have almost completed the 3,200-mile voyage to Tahiti. The weather has been clear and bright, and we have been racing along at the rate of 150 miles per day. The deck has been covered in tortoises brought onboard during our stay in the Galápagos Islands. Unfortunately, most of them are destined to become soup to feed the crew. We have passed rings of coral called lagoon islands. They have long, bright white beaches. It is a wonder the way that they rise so suddenly out of the vast ocean. Mr. Darwin spent a long time looking at them, but he has vanished into his cabin. I am sure he already has his books spread out on the table and is trying to come up with an explanation for these astonishing formations.

At sunrise this morning we got our first glimpse of Tahiti. All of us have been looking forward to visiting the famous South Sea Islands, charted years ago by the great Captain Cook. From on deck I could see groves of coconut palms, breadfruit trees, and banana plantations. The breakers crash onto jagged rocks, sending white sea spray high up into the air. It is a scene straight out of a painting. As we sailed closer, I could see the Tahitians approaching in canoes made from hollowed-out trees. Both the men and women are tattooed and wear garlands of coconut leaves around their heads. The women also have flowers in their hair.

After breakfast, several of us rowed ashore. Both Captain Fitzroy and Mr. Darwin joined the party. We walked along a path through the palms. Huts were dotted among the trees, and we could see the families going about their business. Some were using banana leaves as plates. Over the next few days Mr. Fitzroy took measurements of the coast. Some of us accompanied Mr. Darwin on a trip into the interior of the island. We climbed steep slopes, needing to edge along narrow paths. At one point magnificent waterfalls, 200 to 300 feet high, cascaded around us. Nowhere on our journey have any of us seen more magnificent scenery. We ate roasted bananas and also sampled pineapples and coconut milk. Mr. Darwin thought it was very refreshing, although I wasn't so sure about the taste. I prefer my milk from a cow.

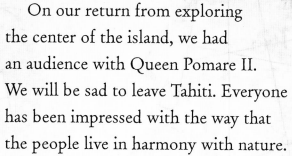

The ship's artist sketched these palm trees.

On our return from exploring the center of the island, we had an audience with Queen Pomare II. We will be sad to leave Tahiti. Everyone has been impressed with the way that the people live in harmony with nature.

So here we are on the far side of the world. Soon, we will turn back toward England and make our way home. I think that Mr. Darwin is growing homesick.

He is reading and rereading the letters that he has received from his sisters at our many ports of call. I think he is dreaming of his family home in Shrewsbury. Little wonder. It is four long years since we first left Plymouth. He is dreaming of England, the stories he is going to tell, and the book he is going to write. The closer we come to the end of the *Beagle*'s voyage, the more I think that Mr. Darwin must have changed his mind about entering the Church. With every day that passes, he is drawn more to the attractions of a scientific life. He has sent so many boxes back to England on our journey and written so many pages of notes. Can he really turn his back on them and settle into the life of a country priest? I just don't believe it. He wants to be a geologist and naturalist.

It is even rumored that Captain Fitzroy is preoccupied with thoughts of home. How I envy these gentlemen their family estates, mothers, fathers, brothers, and sisters. How I would love to have a family of my own to return to. An orphan myself, the moment I return to England I will be looking to sign up for another few years at sea. While Mr. Darwin will have his studies, I have nothing to keep me in England, no ties at all. The vast ocean is my home.

In the four years of our voyage so far, all of us have changed. I am 14 now and both stronger and wiser. Mr. Darwin was 22 when he first boarded the *Beagle*. He is now in his 26th year. He seems to have decided that his hunting and shooting days are behind him. It takes up time that he could be spending on other things. Surely that is another sign that he is going to devote the rest of his life to the study of nature.

Captain Fitzroy has given further encouragement to Mr. Darwin's future career as nature's historian by suggesting that he publishes his diary. Mr. Darwin seems very proud to have been asked. He has also received good news from home in his sisters' letters. The fossils that he sent back are being studied. Scientific men want to meet him. He is becoming quite a celebrity, and I am sure that he has a great future ahead of him.

WHAT HAPPENED NEXT?

From Tahiti, the *Beagle* sailed to New Zealand and then onward to Australia, where Darwin met some of the land's Aboriginal people. He went on to explore coral reefs around the Cocos Islands—also called the Keeling Islands. From there, the *Beagle* continued as far as Mauritius and South Africa before turning home.

The ship arrived in Falmouth, England, on October 2, 1836, almost five years since it had left England. On the way home, Darwin felt that the fields of England were greener than he remembered them. Feeling homesick, he left the ship as soon as the gangplank was down. He walked through the door of his Shrewsbury home, The Mount, three days later on Wednesday, October 5.

The Beagle approaching the port of St. Louis in Mauritius in April 1836.

The notes that Darwin made on the Beagle voyage were the basis for his book, Journal of Researches. *This book is now called* The Voyage of the Beagle.

Five years is a long time to be away from home. Darwin was changing, and he came home to a Great Britain that was changing, too. Railroads were spreading across the country. There were new factories springing up, and the cities were growing. In June 1837, the Victorian era began as 18-year-old Queen Victoria, who would go on to reign for 64 years, came to the throne.

When Darwin left Plymouth, England, in 1831, he was still thinking that he might have a career in the Church. By the time he returned, he believed in God but he wasn't sure that the Old Testament told the whole truth about how the world had been created. Influenced by what he had seen on his travels, he was slowly starting to collect his ideas. One day they would cause a great storm. People still argue about these ideas today.

People were fascinated by Darwin the traveler, and he attended many meetings with scientists. On January 29, 1839, he married his cousin, Emma, with whom he would have a large family. That same year his first book *Journal of Researches* was published as the third volume of Captain Robert Fitzroy's official account of the voyage. It was soon published on its own, and it made Darwin famous. The *Beagle*'s adventures caught the imagination of Victorian England. But Darwin wasn't content to describe the wonders of the natural world, he wanted to explain them.

This was his famous theory of evolution.

This portrait of Emma Darwin was made in 1840. Emma was the granddaughter of Josiah Wedgwood, who was Charles Darwin's uncle and also famous for his pottery.

Darwin's Zoology of the Voyage of HMS Beagle was published in five parts between 1838 and 1843. This illustration from the book shows Darwin's mouse, one of the many new species that Darwin found during his travels.

When Darwin set off on his great journey across the world, most people believed that animals and plants were the way they had always been, created according to God's design. Darwin challenged this and instead said that living creatures were always changing and developing. Life was a struggle for survival. There was no great plan; the changes happened by chance. Those members of each living species that were best suited to their environment would pass on their traits to the next generation, leading to a gradual change of the species. Darwin saw proof of this in his famous finches. From one original type of finch, a variety of different species would evolve through competition and come to live more successfully in their local environment.

A vegetarian finch from the Galápagos Islands. This picture appeared in Darwin's Zoology of the Voyage of HMS Beagle.

Darwin didn't rush to publish his ideas. His most famous book *On the Origin of Species* didn't come out until November 24, 1859, more than 20 years after the *Beagle*'s return. The book caused a sensation and upset many Christians, who believed it challenged the idea of a human soul. Captain Fitzroy was one of the people who opposed Darwin.

The Galápagos finches have different beaks, depending on the food that they eat. Darwin saw this as proof that the birds had adapted to their habitat so that they could survive. This illustration was published in Darwin's Journal of Researches.

LARGE GROUND FINCH   MEDIUM GROUND FINCH   SMALL TREE FINCH   WARBLER FINCH

Darwin suffered from several bouts of illnesses, but that didn't stop him from producing more books that developed his theory of evolution. The idea that upset people the most was that humans were the result of gradual changes from their ape ancestors. Darwin died on April 19, 1882 at the age of 73. He had become one of the most famous men of his time. He was given a large funeral at Westminster Abbey in London, England, where he is buried.

In the years after Darwin's death, most scientists came to believe his views. Many people who believe in God argue that there can still be a creator who designed nature. The argument will go on and on, but Charles Darwin changed the way that we think about the world we live in.

Darwin took a walk around his garden each day. This portrait was taken in the garden of his home, Down House, in 1881.

Charles and Emma Darwin and their eight children lived in Down House in the southeast of England from 1842 until Darwin's death in 1882. The house is now a museum, and many artifacts from Darwin's Beagle voyage can be seen there.

HMS BEAGLE

This is the story of one of the most famous ships that ever sailed the seas. HMS *Beagle* was known as a brig, which is a sailing ship with two square-rigged masts. Brigs were fast and easy to maneuver, and they were similar to the ships seen in pirate movies today. The *Beagle* weighed 242 tons and carried ten guns, though it only carried six during the famous second voyage when Darwin made his discoveries. It was 90 feet in length (around 30m). That is only slightly longer than a tennis court, so it must have been very cramped onboard with a crew of 74.

The crew of the HMS Beagle *was painted by Augustus* Earle *around 1833. All 74 members of the crew are there during a Bible reading in the gunroom.*

HMS *Beagle* was launched in 1820 from Woolwich dockyard on the Thames River in London, England. Nothing in the ship's early life hinted at the fame to come. It spent five years in reserve, waiting to be sent on a voyage. During this time, it was moored without masts or rigging. Eventually, in 1825, it was employed as a survey ship.

This sketch of the inside of the Beagle in 1832 is based on a sketch by Midshipman King. He and Darwin slept in the chart room (top left).

WHALE BOAT

CHART ROOM

MAIN MAST

CAPTAIN'S STOREROOM

CAPTAIN'S CABIN

GUNROOM

MIDSHIPMEN'S BERTH

BREAD ROOM

MIZZENMAST

In May 1826, it set sail to the southern coast of South America, during which Robert Fitzroy took charge of the HMS *Beagle*. He brought four Fuegians back to England, one of whom died after arriving in England in 1830. Fitzroy captained the second *Beagle* voyage (1831–1836), which brought the Fuegians home.

Before the *Beagle* set off on the famous second voyage, Captain Fitzroy arranged for it to be rebuilt—it was in very poor condition. The repairs almost amounted to more than it cost to build the ship originally, but Fitzroy wanted the ship to be in good shape for the voyage through the rough seas around the southern coast of South America. At his own expense, he also used the most up-to-date instruments to help him on the voyage. This included 22 chronometers, which would help him navigate the seas, and five sympiesometers, which were like thermometers and barometers combined and helped Fitzroy judge the weather. Fitzroy later became a pioneer of accurate weather forecasting.

HMS Beagle *in 1841, painted during the third voyage while surveying Australia.*

The third voyage of the *Beagle*, from 1837 to 1843, took it back to Australia, to survey the coast, and to Timor. Her captain named an area of north Australia Port Darwin, after the naturalist.

The ship was later used to control smuggling in the Thames estuary, in the U.K. She was finally sold to scrap merchants and broken up in 1870.

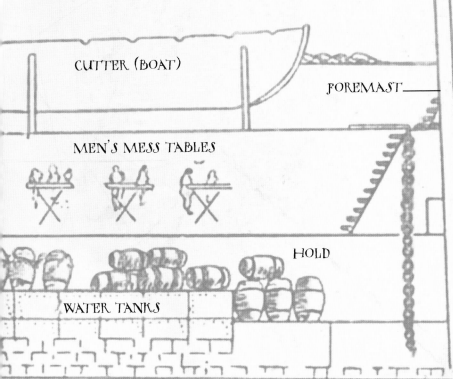

CUTTER (BOAT)

FOREMAST

MEN'S MESS TABLES

HOLD

WATER TANKS

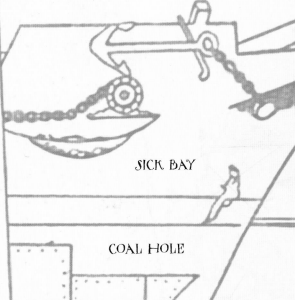

SICK BAY

COAL HOLE

THE ROUTE OF DARWIN'S VOYAGE

Darwin traveled on the second HMS *Beagle* voyage. Today we are used to traveling around the world by airplane, so it is hard to imagine what an amazing journey it must have been. It lasted almost five years, from December 1831 to October 1836, and took in South America, the Falkland Islands, the Galápagos Islands, Tahiti, New Zealand, Australia, and South Africa.

When anybody mentions the second voyage of the *Beagle* today, they usually think about Darwin's scientific discoveries, but it was originally meant to produce naval charts for war or trade. Captain Fitzroy surveyed the coasts of Patagonia (the southern coasts of Chile and Argentina) using smaller boats as well as the *Beagle* so that he could chart the small inlets and rivers that the *Beagle* was too large to survey.

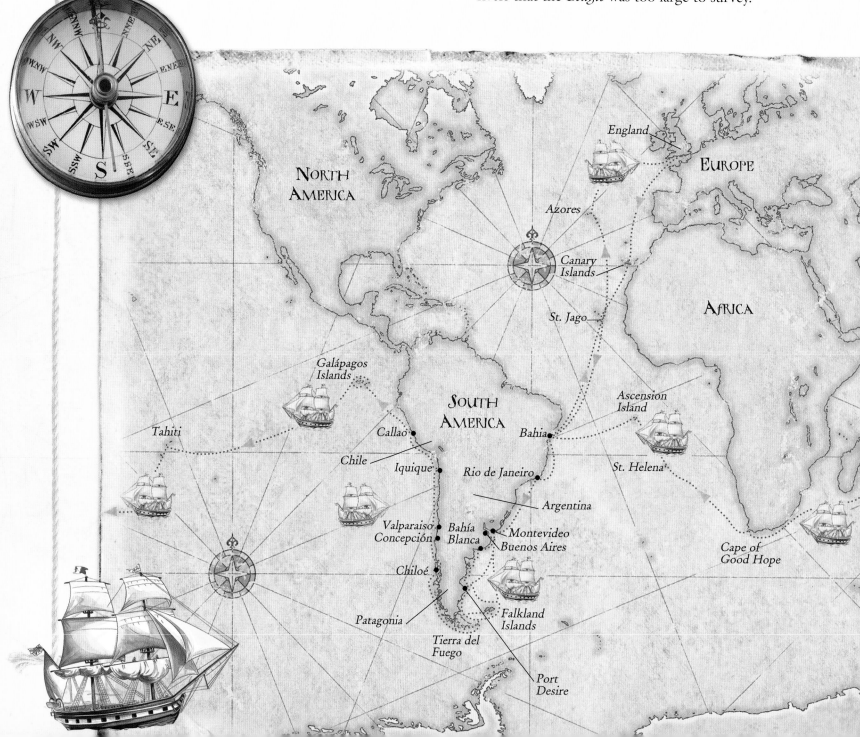

It was a dangerous journey because the seas could be very rough, especially in the cold waters around Tierra del Fuego. There were many islands and rocks to maneuver around and fearsome winds and large waves that could rise up from out of nowhere. Whether for Fitzroy's thorough survey of the region or for Darwin's achievements, this voyage on the *Beagle* is an epic journey that will always be remembered.

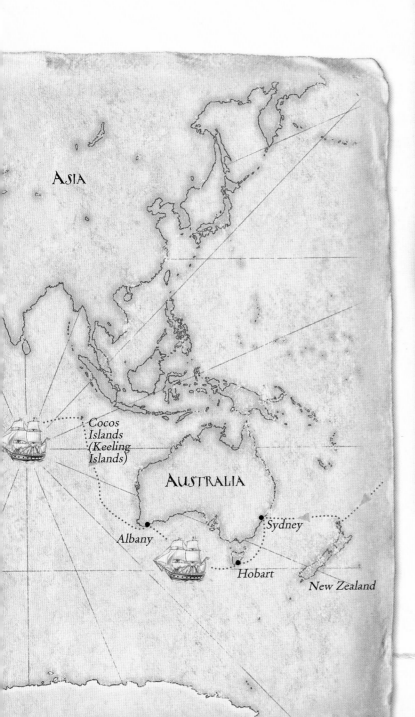

ASIA

Cocos Islands (Keeling Islands)

AUSTRALIA

Albany

Sydney

Hobart

New Zealand

KEY EVENTS OF THE *BEAGLE*'S SECOND VOYAGE

1831
September 5: Robert Fitzroy accepts Charles Darwin as naturalist on the voyage
December 27: HMS *Beagle* leaves Plymouth

1832
January 16: Porto Praya, St. Jago
February 17: Crossing the Line
February 28: Bahia, Brazil
April 4: Rio de Janeiro, Brazil
July 26: Buenos Aires, Argentina, where guard ship fires two shots

1833
January 16: the *Beagle* leaves the three Fuegians on Tierra del Fuego
March 1: Falkland Islands
July 24: completes the survey of the Patagonian coast south of Bahía Blanca

1834
February 25: Woollya Cove, Tierra del Fuego, to meet with Jemmy Button
July 22: Valparaiso, Chile, for three months
November 10: *Beagle* surveys southern tip of Chiloé

1835
March 4: anchors at Concepción, Chile, and sees the ruins after the earthquake
September 15: Galápagos Islands
November 15: Matavai Bay, Tahiti
December 21: New Zealand

1836
April 1: Cocos Islands (Keeling Islands)
April 29: Mauritius
May 31: Cape of Good Hope, South Africa
July 8: St. Helena
August 1: Bahia, Brazil
October 2: arrives back in England

LIFE AT SEA

In the 1800s, life on a ship often meant years in cramped conditions away from home and family. The ship's crew became a sailor's family. Life at sea was dangerous, with stormy seas and slippery decks, as well as diseases from rats and other vermin that crept onboard when the ship docked.

Chain of command on the *Beagle*

Robert Fitzroy, the captain, was in charge of the ship. Below him were John Wickham (first lieutenant) and James Sullivan (second lieutenant). Beneath the second lieutenant came Midshipman Philip Gidley King. The term midshipman comes from the parts of the ship where these officers slept. Senior commissioned officers had their quarters in the stern, midshipmen in the middle, or midships, and the ordinary seamen in the forecastle at the front. Other senior men included Robert McCormick (the surgeon), Benjamin Benoe (the assistant surgeon), and George Rowlett (the purser, who was in charge of handling money onboard).

What were the jobs on the ship?

The surgeon was in charge of the men's health, and the parson took care of the religious welfare of the crew. There was also a cook, a boatswain (in charge of the sails), a carpenter, and a quartermaster, who was in charge of navigating the ship. The remaining crew members had to keep watch, handle the sails, and clean the decks.

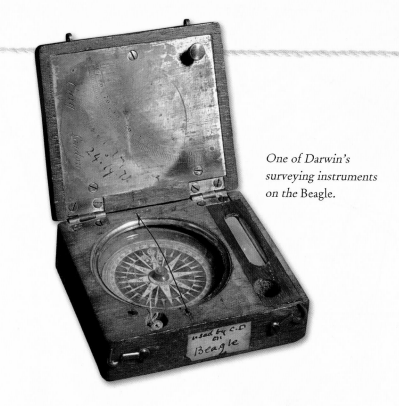

One of Darwin's surveying instruments on the Beagle.

Free time

There was a strong sense of comradeship. The men liked to drink ale together and enjoyed playing dice and cards. They told tales, sang sea chanteys (special songs that were sung by sailors to keep time and rhythm while working), and played music. Some liked carving, practicing tying knots, drawing, and making ship models. When the senior crew members allowed it, the sailors played practical jokes on the officers. This was only on special occasions though, such as Crossing the Line (see page 16). At other times, they could be punished for bad behavior.

Crew members were highly skilled at unfurling sails on the masts and climbing rigging. It was difficult and dangerous work.

Punishment

The captain and his senior officers maintained strict discipline on the ship. Crew members were flogged for misbehaving or put into shackles. The punishments were often carried out in front of everyone on the ship to remind all of the crew members to behave.

Sleeping

The crew slept below deck in hammocks or cradles suspended from the ceiling. They were very close together, and the hammocks rocked from the motion of the ship, which caused Darwin to suffer from seasickness. The hammocks could be rolled up during the day to create more space on the ship.

Health

There was a lot of sickness at sea. The seamen were often cold and wet, and the rats carried diseases. A lack of vitamin C could lead to a disease called scurvy, so the crew had to collect fruit, which is rich in vitamin C, whenever the ship docked. The ship's surgeon took care of any sick crew members in the sick bay.

Food on board

The food on a ship was often of bad quality, and meat, such as pork, was salted so that it would not rot. The seafarers' diet also included cheese, fish, ale, and hard, dry crackers. The crew ate local fresh fruit and meat whenever the ship docked. During the voyage of the *Beagle*, the men ate the animals that they had captured—even the poor tortoises! The tortoises were collected in their hundreds and provided fresh food for the crew to eat while at sea.

The giant tortoises of the Galápagos Islands provided a great meal for the sailors. They were caught and kept onboard to eat during long sea voyages.

DARWIN'S SPECIMENS

All scientists have to collect evidence in order to support their theories. Darwin was away from England for almost five years. In that time he collected an enormous number of specimens of animals, plants, rocks, and fossils.

Collecting methods

In his writing, Darwin describes how he collected his specimens. He lifted up stones and rocks to find the creatures beneath and kept them in jars. Other animals were captured in forests, and many were killed. Sometimes, the animals would be dissected. Darwin also fished for plankton, jellyfish, and other creatures with iron and gauze nets. He would dry plants and keep them in special drying paper. Small creatures were kept in bottles, which Darwin filled with alcohol and chemicals in order to preserve them. The larger animals and fossils were placed into barrels or wooden boxes, which the crew had to make.

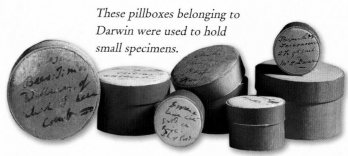
These pillboxes belonging to Darwin were used to hold small specimens.

Identifying specimens

Darwin kept a log book of his specimens, as well as tagging and numbering them all and making notes about the location and time of discovery or capture. Fossilized bones were cleaned and numbered so that they could be assembled correctly back home. In order to help identify his finds, Darwin consulted books that had been written by the experts of the day, and he also wrote to them directly about his discoveries.

A note written by Charles Darwin about evolution. It was through his notes and by examining his specimens that Darwin formed his theories.

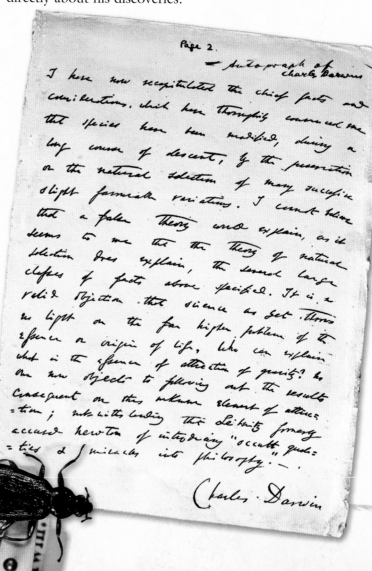

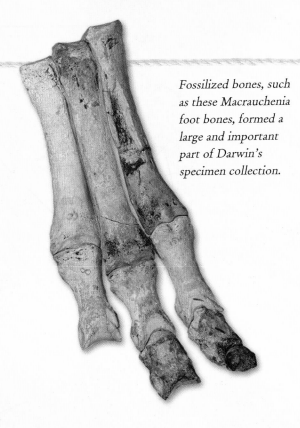

Fossilized bones, such as these Macrauchenia foot bones, formed a large and important part of Darwin's specimen collection.

A man of letters

Whenever the *Beagle* moored by a town, Darwin's letters were sent to England. Ships brought back letters from the finest geologists, zoologists, botanists, and naturalists. It took a long time, but it was a very important way of confirming that he had found a new species.

Sending specimens home

Whenever the *Beagle* interrupted its voyage to allow Darwin to explore, or to make repairs to the ship, the crew would load many boxes and barrels onto ships bound for England. This included the dried plant collections, many jars of preserved creatures, and huge boxes full of fossilized bones, teeth, and skulls. From these remains the scientists back in England would recognize extinct creatures such as the Megatherium and the Hoplophorus.

Specimens collected by Charles Darwin are now held by the Natural History Museum in London, England.

What happened to the specimens?

On Darwin's return to England, he allowed various scientists to take his specimens to study. Some stayed in their cabinets for many years. Eventually, they were sold and donated to great museums such as the Natural History Museum in London, England.

19TH-CENTURY SCIENTISTS

Darwin was one of many important 19th-century scientists. This was a time of great scientific inventions and discoveries. There were significant achievements in mathematics, biology, chemistry, astronomy, physics, and medicine.

Questioning the world

The naturalists of the 1800s collected information in order to investigate how the world worked. There were many theories, and often there were disagreements within the scientific community, but their discoveries ultimately paved the way for a greater understanding of our planet.

Sir Charles Lyell (1797–1875) was a Scottish geologist who argued that the changes that happen to Earth occur slowly and gradually over millions of years, not in a series of sudden catastrophes. He is painted here in Down House (Darwin's home), standing between Sir Joseph Hooker (1817–1911), an English botanist and explorer, and Charles Darwin (left).

Swiss-born Louis Agassiz (1807–1873) was a zoologist and geologist who investigated glaciers and the history of the Ice Age. He later settled in the U.S.

The German biologist and physician Ernst Haeckel (1834–1919) named thousands of new species. There are mountains in the U.S. and New Zealand named after him.

Roderick Murchison *(1792–1871) was a Scottish geologist. He investigated the Silurian and Devonian periods, which are geological time periods in Earth's history.*

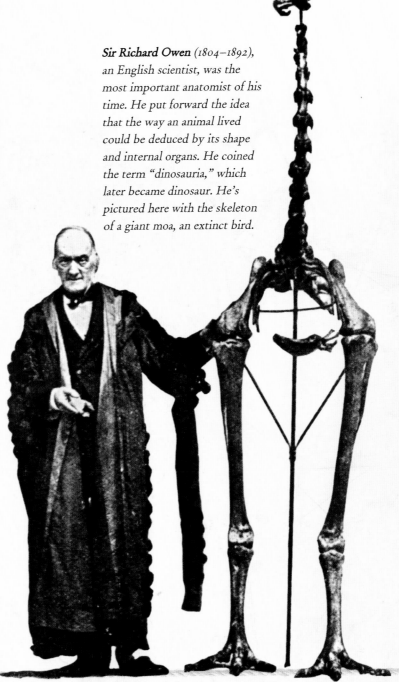

Sir Richard Owen (1804–1892), an English scientist, was the most important anatomist of his time. He put forward the idea that the way an animal lived could be deduced by its shape and internal organs. He coined the term "dinosauria," which later became dinosaur. He's pictured here with the skeleton of a giant moa, an extinct bird.

There were many other eminent biologists and geologists in the 1800s.

Georges Cuvier (1769–1832) was a French scientist, known as the father of vertebrate paleontology. He classified living and fossilized creatures according to their similarities.

Jean-Baptiste Lamarck (1744–1829), a French scientist, was an early believer in the idea that evolution developed according to natural laws. He was a pioneer of botany and biology.

Othniel Charles Marsh (1831–1899) was an American professor of paleontology at Yale University in Connecticut. He discovered around 80 new types of dinosaurs, demonstrating the huge variety of fossil life.

MORE 19TH-CENTURY SCIENTISTS

A changing era

The era in which Darwin lived was a time of great change. As the naturalist and geologist strove to understand the creatures and history of the planet, other scientists were making progress in medicine, electricity technology, and astronomy. New inventions in the form of machines and processes started to make changes to people's lives, from pasteurized milk to electric lighting.

Michael Faraday (1791–1867) was an English chemist and physicist. He studied electricity and magnetism. He discovered benzene and invented an early form of the Bunsen burner.

The French chemist **Louis Pasteur** *(1822–1895) made important discoveries in microbiology. He created the first vaccine for rabies and developed the process of pasteurization to stop milk from turning sour.*

Hermann von Helmholtz (1821–1894) was a German physicist and physician. He made important discoveries in physiology and electromagnetism.

There were many other eminent 19th-century physicists, mathematicians, and astronomers.

Joseph Henry (1797–1878) was an American scientist who became the first secretary of the Smithsonian Institution. He worked in the field of electromagnetism.

German-born **Caroline Herschel** (1750–1848) worked with her brother Sir William Herschel as an astronomer. She discovered several comets and cataloged many stars.

Sofia Kovalevsky (1850–1891) was the first major female Russian mathematician, also known as Sonia Kovalevsky.

William Thomson, Lord Kelvin (1824–1907) was an Irish-born physicist and engineer who did important work in physics. He developed the Kelvin scale of temperature measurement.

*This was a time when few women became scientists. The woman pictured here, **Maria Mitchell** (1818–1889), was the first female professional astronomer in the U.S. In the U.K., **Mary Somerville** (1780–1872) and **Caroline Herschel** (1750–1848) were leading figures in astronomy and the first women to become members of the Royal Astronomical Society.*

EXTINCT CREATURES

The idea of extinction (species dying out completely) was accepted only in the late 1700s. It is caused by many things such as hunting or loss of habitat. Darwin's theory of evolution explained that extinction is a part of natural selection—in which, over time, some animals adapt and survive, others decline in numbers, and some become extinct. Some extinct animals are shown here. A mass extinction around 65 million years ago, most likely because of a meteor impact, wiped out around 50 percent of the world's species (including the dinosaurs) in a short time.

Trilobite
When: 542–250 million years ago
Where: worldwide
Size: average 1–3 in. (2–7cm) long
Diet: Some of these creatures were scavengers. Some swam and fed on plankton.

Hyracotherium (Hyrax beast)
When: around 50 million years ago
Where: Asia, Europe, North America
Size: average 2 ft. (60cm) long
Diet: leaves
This was the earliest member of the horse family. It was the size of a hare and had teeth designed for eating leaves from bushes.

Phorusrhacos (Terror bird)
When: 27 million–15,000 years ago
Where: South America
Size: 8 ft. (2.5m) tall
Diet: large animals
A fast runner, this bird could outrun most of its prey. It was a type of giant, flesh-eating ostrich.

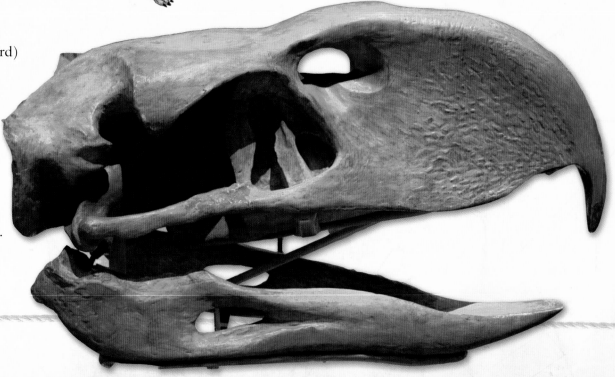

Macrauchenia (Big llama)
When: 7 million–10,000 years ago
Where: South America
Size: 6.5 ft. (2m) tall
Diet: ground plants
This animal was long legged,
long necked, and had a trunk.

Smilodon
(Saber-toothed tiger)
When: 2.5 million–
10,000 years ago
Where: North America
and South America
Size: 6.5 ft. (2m) long
Diet: big mammals
This animal evolved to kill
the big plant eaters of the time.

Glyptodon
When: 2.5 million–
10,000 years ago
Where: North America
and South America
Size: around 10 ft.
(3m) long
Diet: low plants
This was a large
armadillo-like animal
from South America.

Megatherium
When: 2 million–
8,000 years ago
Where: North,
Central, and South
America
Size: 10 ft. (3m) tall
Diet: trees
This was a giant
sloth that evolved
in South America.

GLOSSARY

anatomist
A person who studies the body structures of plants or animals.

astronomer
A scientist who studies the stars and the universe.

barometer
An instrument used to measure air pressure.

benefactor
A person who helps another, especially by giving money.

berth
A cabin on a ship.

botanist
A scientist who studies plants.

bow
A name for the front of a ship.

brig
A type of ship that is fast and easy to maneuver.

cat-o'-nine-tails
A whip with nine knotted rope or leather ends.

caulk
To seal and make watertight the wooden planks of a ship.

chart
To make a note of coastlines, currents, and sea depths to create a sea map (also called a chart).

Crossing the Line
A ceremony on a ship to celebrate a person's first crossing of the equator. The event is overseen by a person dressed as Neptune, the king of the sea. Traditionally, the ship's officers let the sailors take over for the duration of the ceremony.

dissect
To take something apart in order to see the internal workings.

embedded
Stuck firmly inside something.

equator
An imaginary line around the center of Earth, which runs through the tropical (hot and usually wet) regions.

evolution
The process of change from one generation to the next.

extinct
When all animals of a species die, and none are left.

finch
A type of small bird. Darwin studied the many different finch species in the Galápagos Islands.

flogging
Whipping with the end of a rope or a cat-o'-nine-tails.

forecastle
The part of the ship, above and below deck, that is in front of the foremast.

fossil
The remains of ancient animals or plants that have turned to rock.

gaucho
A cowboy of the South American pampas.

gauze
A thin, see-through fabric. When used in a net, it allows water to drain, leaving creatures behind.

geologist
A scientist who studies the surface, life, and history of Earth.

hereditary
Passed down from one generation to the next such as from parents to their children.

Hoplophorus
A type of Glyptodon, which was a large, armadillo-like animal.

instrument maker
The instrument maker onboard the HMS *Beagle* was employed by the captain to take care of the ship's navigational equipment.

Mastodon
An elephant-like animal that lived in Europe, Asia, and North America thousands of years ago.

Megatherium
A type of elephant-size ground sloth that lived in the Americas from two million to 8,000 years ago.

missionary
A person sent on a mission, especially to do religious or charitable work.

naturalist
A scientist who studies living things.

paleontology
The study of prehistoric life through the examination of fossils.

pampas
The vast, flat grasslands of lowland South America.

parasite
A plant or animal living on or feeding off another living thing and doing it harm.

physicist
A scientist who studies the forces of Earth such as electricity and heat.

pioneer
Someone who opens up a new area of thought or research or who goes into unknown areas.

plankton
Tiny sea animals or plants that float in the ocean and are the main food for many sea animals.

preserve
To keep from rotting.

rigging
The network of ropes that helps hold up a ship's masts and allows its sails to be controlled.

sanctuary
A safe place.

scurvy
A disease of the skin and gums caused by a lack of vitamin C.

sea chantey
A rhythmic song that helped sailors pass their day-to-day activities on a ship.

shackled
Chained up using a type of heavy chain called a shackle.

stern
The rear of a ship.

surveying
Measuring an area of land, such as a coastline, to make a map of it.

tamarind
A sour tropical fruit that grows in Africa and Asia.

theory
A scientist's explanation of something.

thumbscrew
An instrument of torture used by some slave owners in the 1800s. It slowly crushed a person's thumbs.

trawl
A wide-mouthed net that is dragged through the water to catch creatures.

vermin
Small animals and insects that do harm—for example by carrying diseases.

vertebrate
An animal that has an internal skeleton.

INDEX

ACKNOWLEDGMENTS

The publisher would like to thank the following for permission to reproduce their material. Every care has been taken to trace copyright holders. However, if there have been unintentional omissions or failure to trace copyright holders, we apologize and will, if informed, endeavor to make corrections in any future edition.

Key: *b* = bottom, *c* = center, *l* = left, *r* = right, *t* = top

Pages 2*tr* English Heritage/Down House, Kent, England; 2*cr* Science Photo Library (SPL)/Barbara Strnadova; 2*br* Natural History Museum, London, England; 4*tl* English Heritage/Down House, Kent; 4*l* iStockphoto; 4*bc* Natural History Museum, London; 4*br* Natural History Museum, London; 8 iStockphoto; 8*tr* Natural History Museum, London; 13*r* Getty/Dorling Kindersley; 14*t* Natural History Museum, London; 14*cl* Oxford University of Natural History/Darwin database; 15*tr* National Maritime Museum, London, England; 15*cr* National Maritime Museum, London; 16*l* iStockphoto; 17*tr* Frank Lane Picture Agency/Ronald Thompson; 18*tr* Natural History Museum, London; 22*tl* Lyndon Baines Johnson Library and Museum, Austin, Texas; 22*cl* Photolibrary/Christopher Fairweather; 24 Natural History Museum, London; 26*cl* Corbis/David Stoecklein; 27*t* Bridgeman Art Library/Giraudon; 27*r* Photolibrary/Steve Cole; 32*cl* Alamy/Andrew Linscott; 33*cr* Heritage Image Partnership (HIP)/Ann Ronan Picture Library; 33*br* UBC Botanical Garden and Centre for Plant Research, Vancouver, Canada; 34*cl* iStockphoto; 34*br* Natural History Museum, London; 36 Alamy/David Frazier; 38*lc* University of Cambridge; 42 Alamy/Mary Evans Picture Library; 43*t* Bridgeman Art Library/Down House; 43*b* Natural History Museum, London; 44*tl* Alamy/Natural History Museum, London; 44*b* Bridgeman Art Library/Down House; 45*tl* Natural History Museum, London; 45*tr* Bridgeman Art Library; 45*r* HIP/Ann Ronan Picture Library; 45*b* Corbis/David Ball; 46*tr* National Maritime Museum, London; 48 English Heritage/Down House; 48–49 iStockphoto; 50 English Heritage/Down House; 51 Alamy/fotoNatura; 52*tr* English Heritage/Down House; 52*c* Natural History Museum, London; 52*br* Getty/Hulton; 52*c*, 53*tl* Natural History Museum, London; 52*c*, 53*br* Natural History Museum, London; 54*tr* Bridgeman Art Library; 54*c* SPL/Marine Biological Laboratory; 54*bl* Getty/Hulton; 55*tl* Corbis/Hulton; 55*b* SPL/George Bernard; 56*l* Getty/Time Life; 56*tr* Getty/Hulton; 56*br* Heidelberg University, Germany; 57*tr* SPL/Royal Astronomical Society; 57*br* Science & Society Picture Library; 58*tr* Natural History Museum, London; 58*cl* Natural History Museum, London; 59*tl* Natural History Museum, London; 59*c* Natural History Museum, London; 59*br* Natural History Museum, London; 64 Ardea